AMAZING MR. PELGREW

By Miriam Schlein
Illustrated by Harvey Weiss

Steven and Mr. Pelgrew were good friends, and Steven told him about what happened near at home and Mr. Pelgrew would tell Steven what happened in town. Sometimes he rescued a duck, helped trucks move, scared crows. What did Mr. Pelgrew do, wondered Steven? He just had to find out!

* *

Dewey Decimal Classification: Fic

Amazing Mr. Pelgrew

by Miriam Schlein

illustrated by Harvey Weiss

1962 FIRST CADMUS EDITION
THIS SPECIAL EDITION IS PUBLISHED BY ARRANGEMENT WITH
THE PUBLISHERS OF THE REGULAR EDITION
ABELARD-SCHUMAN LIMITED
BY
E. M. HALE AND COMPANY
EAU CLAIRE, WISCONSIN

Steven lived in a little house outside of town. One day Mr. Pelgrew moved in next door. And even though Steven was a little boy and Mr. Pelgrew was a great big man, Steven and Mr. Pelgrew got to be very good friends.

Steven and Mr. Pelgrew used to go for walks across the fields. Sometimes they came to a fence. Steven was so small that he could crawl right *under* the fence, and Mr. Pelgrew was so big that he could step right *over* the fence.

But that didn't matter. In fact it was fine! Because Steven went under and Mr. Pelgrew stepped over, and still they were very good friends.

Steven knew a lot about little
things right near home—like
mushrooms in the fields, and birds' nests,
and moles digging holes, and
buttercups growing all over the hill.

Mr. Pelgrew knew more about the exciting things that went on in town. Because Mr. Pelgrew went off to town to work every day, and saw everything there was to see, while Steven stayed at home.

But that didn't matter. In fact it was fine! Because then Steven could tell Mr. Pelgrew about things that happened near-at-home, and Mr. Pelgrew could tell Steven about things that went on in town.

And Steven and Mr. Pelgrew were really *very* good friends.

One night after supper, when the
sun was sliding behind the hills, Steven
ran over to Mr. Pelgrew's house to help
Mr. Pelgrew feed his rabbits. (And
that was another reason why Steven
and Mr. Pelgrew were such good friends.
They both loved rabbits—pink-eared,
twitchy-nosed, fluffy bunny rabbits.)

And Steven said, "Mr. Pelgrew,
what did you do at work today, when
you went to town?"

Mr. Pelgrew said, "I did lots of
things, but the nicest thing was this.
I saw a snow-white duck walking across
Main Street, right in the middle of the
cars and the trucks and the stores and
all the people. The poor little duck
didn't know where he was, or where to go,
and how to get back to the farm where
he lived—and he looked oh so scared
because he was lost.

"So I picked him up and held him tight, and took him right over to Mr. Jiggle's Petshop, and Mr. Jiggle took one look and said, 'Why, that's Freddy, Mrs. Fluff's pet duck. Mrs. Fluff has been looking for him all morning, and she will be very glad to see him. I will call her right now, to tell her I have her duck.'

"That is what Mr. Jiggle said—and as I left, the duck looked at me and said SCRAW SCRAW—and *you* know what it means when a duck says SCRAW. He was saying, 'Thank you, Mr. Pelgrew.' Wasn't that nice?"

"Oh," said Steven, "that was very
nice." He gave a piece of lettuce to
a pink-eared rabbit, and thought to
himself, "That is a funny kind of job
Mr. Pelgrew has—to pick up ducks in the
street, and make them happy and safe."

But Steven didn't have a chance
to say this, because suddenly it was
late, and getting dark and chilly,
and he had to go home to bed.

So he just said "Good night," and
Mr. Pelgrew said "Good night."
"Good night, rabbits," they both said.
And they both went into their houses.

The next night when Mr. Pelgrew came home, Steven helped him clear his strawberry patch, and as they cleared the patch Steven said, "What did you do at work today, Mr. Pelgrew?"

Mr. Pelgrew stood up straight to rest his back for a minute and said, "Today was market day, and all the farmers drove into town with trucks and wagons of lettuce and melons and potatoes and squash. Then the streets got crowded and hard to drive through.

"I just helped the drivers get to where they wanted to go, and I saw that all the wagons kept moving along, so they got to market in time."

"Oh," said Steven, "that was nice
of you. Were all the drivers glad
that you helped them to get where
they wanted to go?"

"Well, sometimes yes and sometimes
no, but that is part of my job," said
Mr. Pelgrew.

"Oh, yes," said Steven, and he
imagined himself telling all the
farmers and drivers which way to go.
He liked that idea.

But Steven didn't have a chance to
say this, because he got so tired from
weeding the patch he didn't even
feel like talking.

So he ate a strawberry, and said,
"Good night," and then went home
to bed.

The next day was a holiday, so early in the morning Steven and Mr. Pelgrew went for a walk through the fields.

They came to a fence. There were crows on the fence. When Steven and Mr. Pelgrew came closer, the crows flew away.

Then Steven crawled under the fence and Mr. Pelgrew stepped over the fence, and just as soon as they walked away the crows flew back to the fence.

"Tomorrow," said Steven, "I am
going to help Daddy build a scarecrow
to stand in the field to scare the crows
away. If we don't do this, they will
peck up all the seeds and nothing will
grow—so we will scare the crows with an
old scarecrow—that's what we will do!"

Mr. Pelgrew laughed and said, "Sometimes, in my job in town, I am a kind of scarecrow, too. There I stand—and sometimes just seeing me there helps keep people from doing wrong—just as seeing the scarecrow keeps the crows from pecking the seeds."

"Oh," said Steven, and he was very puzzled, and he thought to himself, "A scarecrow? Is that what Mr. Pelgrew is in the city?

"But a scarecrow doesn't help ducks to go home. A scarecrow doesn't help trucks to move through town. How can Mr. Pelgrew be a scarecrow in town?"

Steven didn't understand at all! And so he just thought, "Well, it's funny, but maybe that's just the way jobs in town are!"

One day, not long after that, Steven's
mother said, "Today, Steven, we are
all going to town."

"Oh," said Steven, "then I will see Mr.
Pelgrew and I will watch him do his job—
although, really, I am not quite sure
what kind of job he does.

"Is he a crow-scarer,

a truck-mover,

a duck-helper—

or what?"

"We will see very soon," said Steven's
mother.

And Steven's daddy smiled as they
rode into town.

The very first minute they got to town,
Steven saw Mr. Pelgrew. Mr. Pelgrew
was standing there, in the middle of
the two busiest streets in town.

And just because Mr. Pelgrew was
holding his hand up high, all the cars and
trucks, and all the men on motorcycles,
and all the boys on bicycles stopped dead
in their tracks!

"Mr. Pelgrew!" cried Steven. "Mr. Pelgrew is a policeman!"

And Steven waved and jumped up and down with excitement.

Mr. Pelgrew saw him and waved back. Then he had to blow a whistle to tell all the cars and trucks, and men on motorcycles, and boys on bicycles, that now they could go, and so Mr. Pelgrew didn't have a chance to talk to Steven at all.

"Oh, my," said Steven, "there is my own friend, Mr. Pelgrew, and he seems to be just about the busiest man in town!"

Steven could hardly wait until he could talk to Mr. Pelgrew.

That night, after supper, Steven ran over to Mr. Pelgrew's house.

Mr. Pelgrew was sitting on the porch with Mrs. Pelgrew, and he was holding the wool for her.

"Oh, Mr. Pelgrew," said Steven, "you didn't tell me you were a policeman!

"Sometimes I used to think you were a duck-finder, or a truck-mover, or a scarecrow, and sometimes I couldn't guess *what* you were.

"But now I know."

Steven shook his head.

"To think that you are a policeman, when at night you are just plain Mr. Pelgrew, my own friend, who lives next door, and loves rabbits, and goes for walks, and has long talks about moles and their holes, and birds flying over the hill, and snowflakes, and how they fall. . . ."

Mr. Pelgrew nodded.

"It is funny," he said, "that I am all those things. In town my job is different every day, and sometimes people must listen to me, and I must tell them what to do, if they are doing wrong.

"But at home, I am not a duck-finder, or a truck-mover, or a scarecrow, or even a policeman.

"At home I am just plain Mr. Pelgrew, and you know, Steven—that is really what I like best to be!"

Then he smiled, and Mrs. Pelgrew smiled, and Steven smiled, too. Then they sat there and watched the sun go down behind the hills—and it was all just the same as any other night. Steven and Mr. Pelgrew were still very good friends.